Ten Little Fish

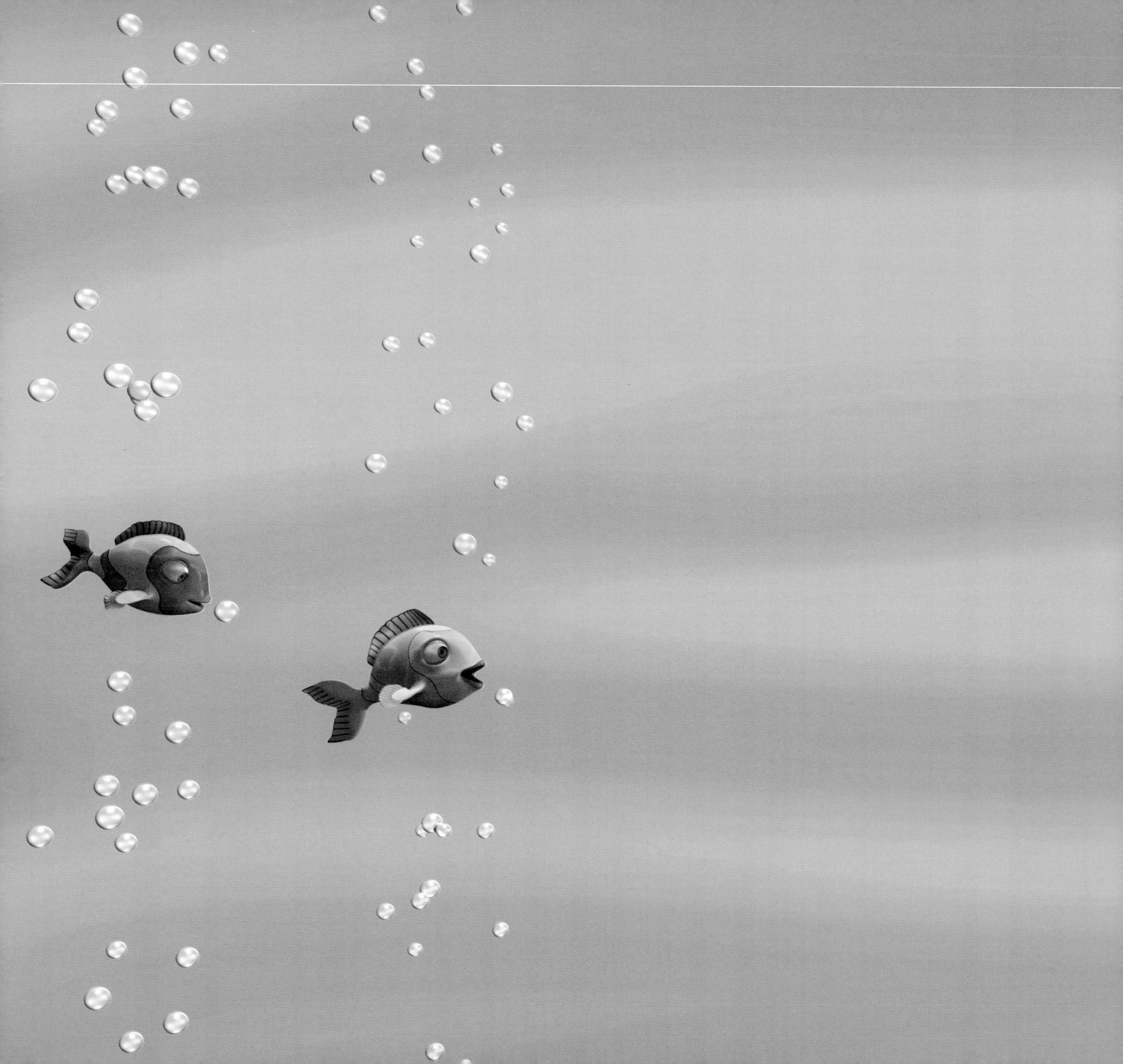

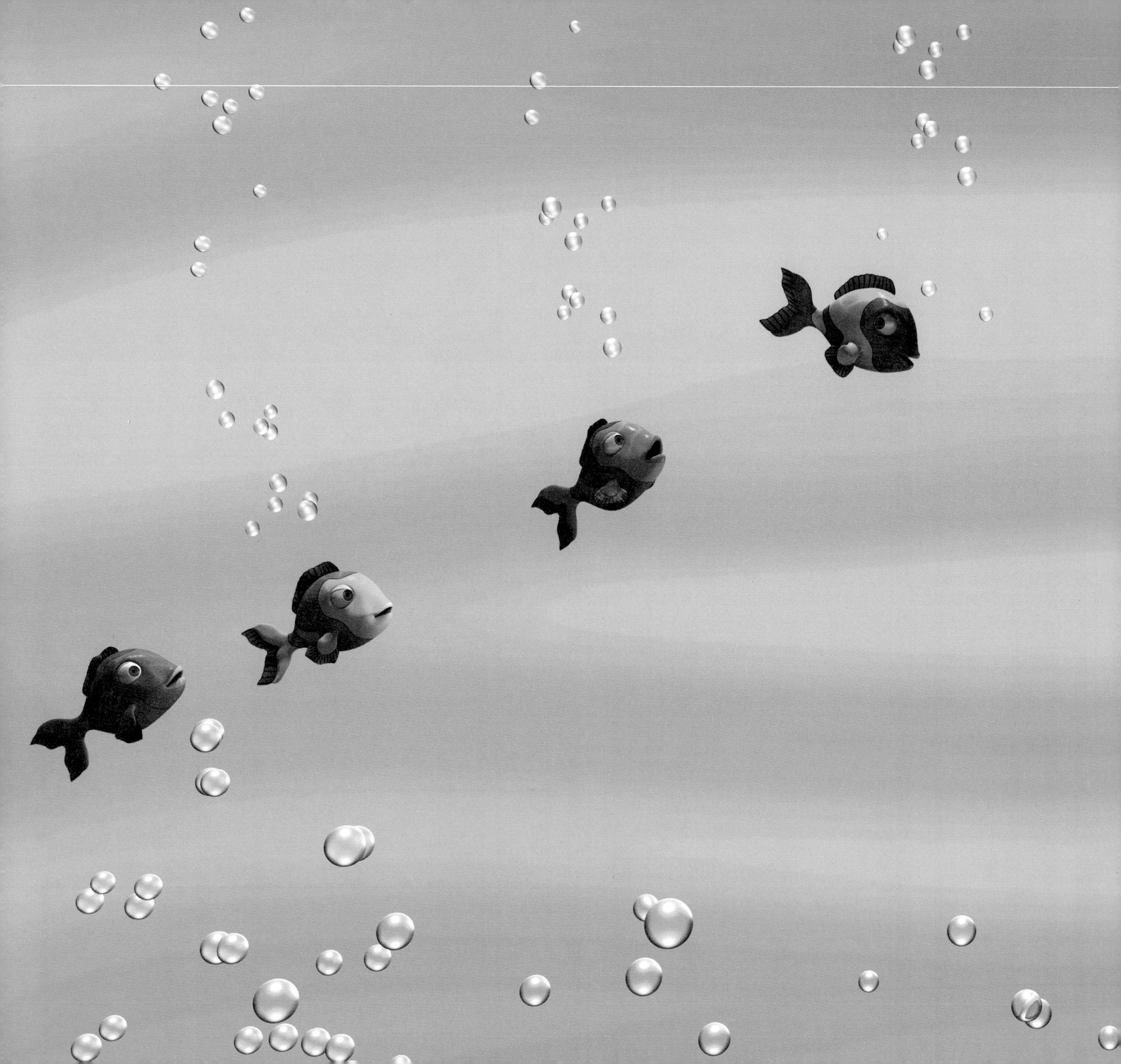

Ten Little Fish

by AUDREY WOOD

illustrated by BRUCE WOOD

SCHOLASTIC INC.

New York Toronto London Auckland Sydney

Mexico City New Delhi Hong Kong Buenos Aires

This book was originally published in hardcover by the Blue Sky Press in 2004.

ISBN 0-439-73870-9

Text copyright © 2004 by Audrey Wood. Illustrations copyright © 2004 by Bruce Wood. All rights reserved.

Published by Scholastic Inc. SCHOLASTIC and associated logos are trademarks and/or registered trademarks of Scholastic Inc.

30 29 28 27 26 25 24 23 22   17 18 19 20 21/0

Printed in the U.S.A.   08

First Scholastic paperback printing, September 2005

The illustrations in this book were created digitally using various 3-D modeling software packages, assisted by Adobe Photoshop.

For Claire Roy

A.W.

For Jason Banks

B.W.

Ten Little Fish, swimming in a line.

One dives down, and now there are . . .

Nine Little Fish, swimming 'round a crate.

One goes in, and now there are . . . .

Eight Little Fish, swimming toward heaven.
One jumps up, and now there are . . .

Seven Little Fish, swimming through sticks.

One gets lost, and now there are . . .

Six Little Fish, swimming to survive.
One likes to hide, and now there are . . .

Five Little Fish, swimming by the shore.
One grabs a snack, and now there are . . .

Four Little Fish, swimming out to sea.
One makes a friend, and now there are . . .

Three Little Fish, swimming in the blue.

One waves good-bye, and now there are . . .

Two Little Fish, swimming in the sun.
One takes a nap, and now there's only . . .

One Little Fish.

What will he do?

Along comes another fish, and that makes . . .

Two Little Fish, in love with each other.

Soon one is a father, and the other is a . . .

Mother!
But Mother and Father don't count this time . . .

Just Ten Little Fish—swimming in a line!

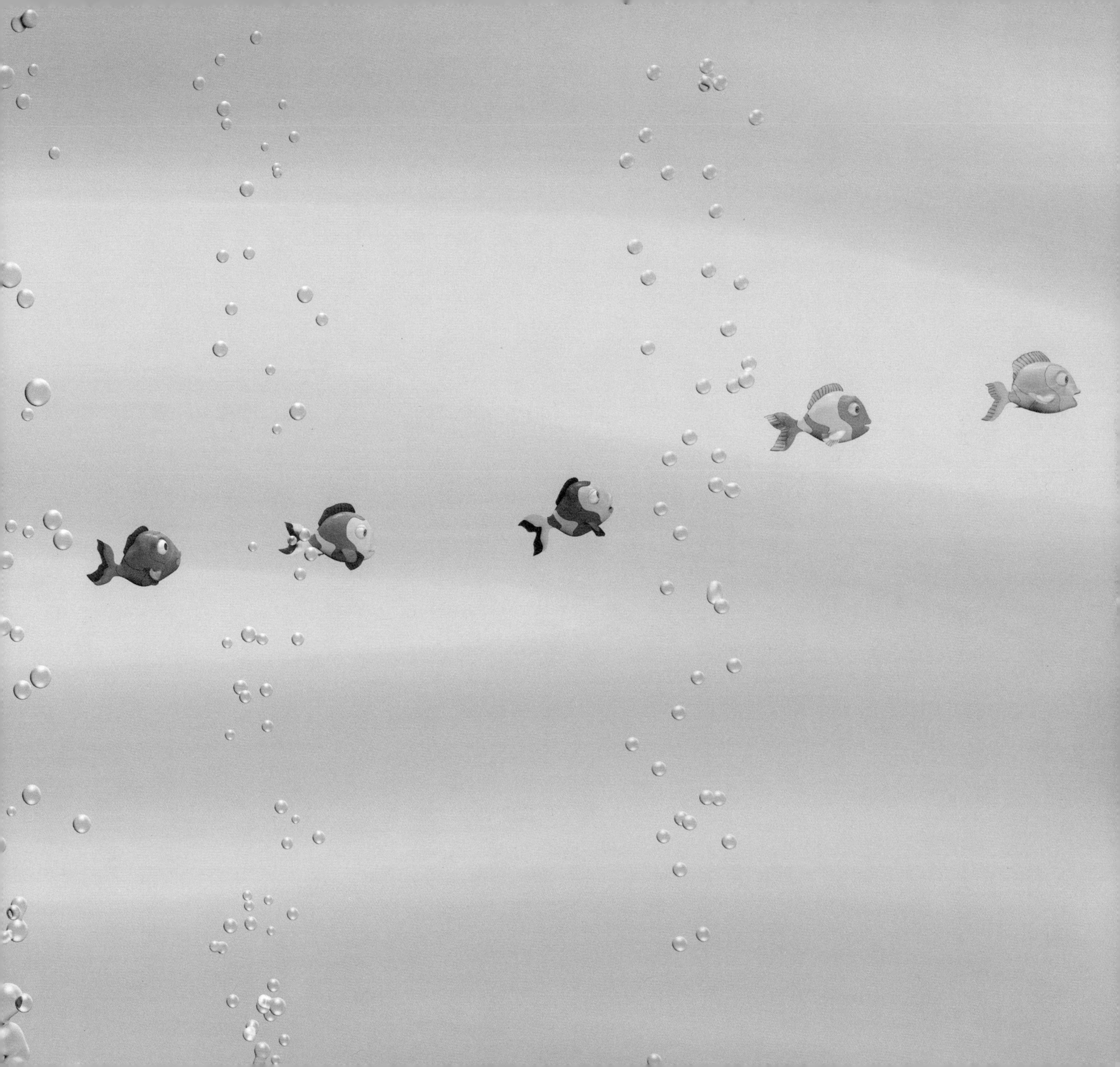